Coinkeeper

The Avery Chronicles

Book 1

By Teresa Schapansky

Coinkeeper
The Avery Chronicles
Copyright © 2021
TNT BOOK PUBLISHING
All rights reserved.

The author may be reached at:
www.teresaschapansky.com
ISBN: 978-1-988024-10-3

DEDICATION

This book is dedicated to all readers between the ages of 0 to 99, that are looking for a quick, entertaining, and perhaps slightly educational, story.

TABLE OF CONTENTS

ACKNOWLEDGMENTS

Most sincere gratitude and appreciation to
the following, for their kind assistance
and very generous contributions for
the purpose of this book:

1911 Canadian Silver Dollar
to the Bank of Canada Museum for the
historical value information, and; to the
Royal Mint Museum for the images

Syilx First Nations
to the Sncəwips Heritage Museum for the
historical and invaluable cultural
information

Coinkeeper

The Avery Chronicles

Book 1

By Teresa Schapansky

BOOK 1

Every person I've ever known made fun of and laughed at my poor, old grandpa. Even my mom, his very own kid, would laugh and call him crazy.

I thought that was mean, but then, I wasn't an adult, so my ideas did not count.

My mom always told me that over and over, again. Always. Like it was my fault, that I was eleven years old.

So, I had a whole lot of ideas that I learned to keep to myself. Because well, if all adults are that mean, I'd like to stay a kid, forever.

Mom said grandpa asked for it. I don't think so. Who would ever ask to be made fun of?

She said it was because of the crazy stories he'd tell.

Also because of how he dressed and how he walked with the clink-clink racket his bag of silly coins made. He always carried that bag on his belt strap.

Grandpa had long grey hair and a long grey beard that reached all the way to his chest. Me? I thought each of those things made him special.

Back to grandpa. I think he liked me best, out of my six brothers and two sisters. Maybe it was because I was the only one that paid attention to him.

But it doesn't matter why. I felt like he was my grandpa and my grandpa only.

Grandpa would come and go when he

wanted. And when he came? He always came home after dark, and I'd know before anyone else.

You see, my bedroom window (well, my shared bedroom - shared with my two little brothers) faced his shed.

My little brothers were way too small to notice things like that. Plus, they were far too short to see out the window.

His shed, you ask? A real nice shed at the edge of our very big back yard. Inside, there was one light bulb.

As soon as that light bulb turned on, I would smile and sneak out my window to visit with him.

Grandpa had the only key to the shed, so I knew it couldn't be anyone else but him.

Grandpa liked to fill my head with stories, and I liked to hear them. I'd rush to the shed and creep open the door, and I'm sure he was always waiting for me to do that.

He'd pat the edge of his bed, and I'd sit right there beside him. Sometimes I would even fall asleep while he spoke.

The way he talked about sword fights and kingdoms and battles and oceans and deserts and Vikings and stuff – he made it sound like he was really there for all of it.

But that could not be possible. It didn't matter, I liked to listen to him, anyway.

On the day that my grandpa left, he paid off my mom's house and gave her so much money that she would never ever have to worry.

Mom said he also went to a lawyer and set up a trust, whatever that means, so that our house would belong to our family forever.

My mom assumed that he'd died, and she said his secrets went to his grave with him. What does she know, anyway? I guess not as much as I know.

You see, just months before he left, I sat with him in the shed. I didn't know that would be one of the last times I would see him there – for a very long time.

Looking back, I am pretty sure he knew. He looked at me long and hard, and he made sure I was looking at him long and hard, too.

"My boy, we are cut from the same cloth." I just kept looking at him, but I think I nodded.

"We are more alike than you know, I'm just older, that's all." He waited for a minute.

"There are things in this world that can't be explained. Not by words, not by history, and not by your teachers at school. Doesn't make those things not real."

I nodded again, and I thought he was warming up to tell me another story.

"If I leave this earth, boy, I will not leave you. I'll be with you in here." He patted his chest where his heart would be.

Then he patted his bag of coins and said, "And I'll also be with you in here." Well, that upset me.

"Grandpa, are you leaving this earth?" I could not even think about life without my grandpa.

We were as close as best friends could be. It didn't matter that he was like one hundred years older than me. He was my person.

"Well, everyone leaves at some point, Avery. We can't ever tell when it's our time to go.

And so, I have to tell you some very secret things that are meant for your ears only." His voice became quieter, then.

"If you tell anyone, *you'll* be made fun of and everyone would call *you* crazy." I guess he should know that better than anyone else in the world, ever would.

I watched as he got up from the bed, and undid his belt strap. In the next moment, he held the bag of silly coins between his old hands.

He put the bag right in front of my face. So close that I think I could smell something burnt. I had never smelled anything like it before.

"Avery, listen up and listen good." Well, I always listened good, but now I listened extra good.

"One day, these will be yours. You take care of them like they are your only child. You hear me?"

Oh, believe me, I heard him loud and clear.

"This bag was given to me by my grandad. It was given to him by his grandpappy. And so the story goes." What story, I wondered. What did that mean?

Like always, grandpa kept on talking, and I kept on listening. I felt like this was the most important visit ever.

"A very, very long time ago, there was a king who felt he owed a large debt to a simple farmer.

The farmer had saved the king's only son from drowning in a creek.

The king knew that no amount of money could ever repay the farmer for his good deed and so he filled a bag with coins and brought them to his wizard."

Man, did I love grandpa's stories.

"The wizard cast a spell on the bag, and the king gave the bag to the farmer. The farmer told the king that he was happy to save the king's son, and that he did not want a reward.

The king insisted and finally the farmer took the bag." I looked with wonder, even closer at the bag.

"Grandpa, is this the very same bag of coins?" He nodded at me. I guess it was not a bag of silly coins, after all.

"It is, Avery." Then, for the first time ever, he held the bag open in front of me.

I peered inside and saw that it was empty. Not even one coin. How could that be?

"We don't pick the coins. The coins pick us. If I reached into the bag right now, I would have a coin in my hand. Never the same coin, mind you.

This old bag is a gift or it is a curse. Depends on how you want to see it." Then he went back to the story about the farmer.

"You see, the farmer had to keep the coins. Many years later, when he died, one of his sons kept the coins.

And then, when that son died, his first-born son kept the coins. And so the story goes."

Well, I knew that my grandpa did not have a son. His only kid was my mom. And so, if my grandpa ever left this earth, who would keep the coins, then?

I was confused. I think grandpa read my mind.

"It'll be you, Avery. You must keep the coins when I leave this earth. It will be up to you to decide if it is a gift or a curse.

It's kind of like, is your cup half empty, or is it half full?"

Well, I did not know what that meant, but if my grandpa wanted me to keep the coins, that's exactly what I would do.

I did not know then, that I really had no choice in the matter.

"No more serious talk, Avery, we'll have lots of time for that. How was school today?"

I told him how school was, but it was the same every day.

Grandpa didn't seem to ever get tired of me telling him the same old boring story.

I knew that like always, once I was done, it would be his turn to tell me a story. And as always, he didn't disappoint me.

"One of the first times I pulled a coin, it was a 1911 Canadian Silver Dollar, but that's not important now.

My travels took me way back to a time, when the first white people had begun to arrive in the Okanagan Valley, in the early 1800s."

Well, this was a little too much even for me, and for the first time, I wondered if my mom was right.

"Grandpa, how can that be?" I quickly did the math in my head (I was very good at math).

"That would make you over two hundred years old." I already really liked his other stories a lot better than this one.

"Avery," he said sternly. "Let me finish. I already told you that there are things that happen that can't be explained."

I laid back on his pillow and rested my arms behind my head. It seemed like this would be a very long night.

"So, it was during the spring, when I appeared in the valley, and I looked like a poor farmhand.

I wore a long-sleeved brown shirt and baggy trousers held to my waist with an old, worn out rope for a belt.

I looked down at my feet and saw that my scuffed-up boots were big and heavy and I suppose, would keep out the rain if need be.

I slipped the coin into my pocket and carried on my way.

The first people I met were the syilx, a First Nations people.

Although I was not the first white man they'd seen, I think they were surprised to see a white man alone, approaching their village.

The syilx were very welcoming, and I was invited to lodge with them. I learned a lot about their way of life, and gained many life skills during my stay with them.

I learned how to hunt, trap and fish, and I even helped to tan animal hides. I even got my own pair of deer hide moccasins to wear during the summer, and a cozy pair of mukluks for the colder months.

That trip touched my heart more than any other trip before it ever did, and any trip after it, ever would.

Speaking and understanding any other language has never been a problem.

It is part of the things that happen, that we can't explain.

Because the white people were very new to the valley, I would help the syilx and the white people speak with each other.

I guess you could say that I had quite eagerly become their translator.

Right away, I noticed that the syilx were very peaceful, not just with each other, but with everyone they'd meet.

The syilx people lived in qwiċi houses (pronounced, "kwee-ts-hee") from fall until summer.

These pine-framed homes were partly built under the ground. Did you know that pine works to drive away insects?

The upper parts of these houses would be covered with dirt. Grass would then grow from the dirt, which added a needed layer of insulation.

I learned how to build these, too." Something did not sound right to me.

"But grandpa, you said from fall until summer. Where did they live the rest of the year?"

"The territory of the syilx was huge; there was nearly 69,000 square kilometres of land to make use of.

From summer to fall, they moved around on their land, spending time gathering and eating foods that only grew during those warmer months."

"What kinds of foods were those?" I asked.

"Well, when I was with them, we picked roots, berries, nuts, seeds, wild celery and onion, and the mushrooms that are safe to eat. Not all mushrooms are edible, Avery.

This time was also spent fishing for salmon, and hunting deer, goat, rabbit, beaver, porcupine, moose and elk.

I learned how to skin and butcher, and the most important part was getting the meats ready to store all winter long."

"Grandpa, what do you mean, store it? Do you mean in the fridge or freezer?" I didn't know they had those things way back then.

"The same idea, Avery, except there was no such thing as fridges or freezers.

The meats would be cut, then dried in the sun, and once ready, set in boxes made of pine. Do you remember that pine keeps insects away?" I did.

"The pine boxes, we would bury six feet into the ground.

That way, the meat stayed cool enough to last over the winter, and the boxes were deep enough to keep bears from finding the meat.

We even lit fires to protect and control the land. Have you ever heard of a prescribed burn?" I shook my head, no.

"Well, this is a method of burning parts of the land in a controlled way."

"But grandpa, why would anyone light a fire on purpose?" I had always been told, even by grandpa, not to play with fire.

"This was done for many reasons, like to clean up the forest floor to make room for new plant growth, and animal homes, or habitats.

Also, by burning a path through the land, there was a much better chance of taming or controlling natural fires.

Prescribed burning is even nowadays,

very common, Avery. I just didn't know that this was practiced even way back then.

And so, during those months, the syilx lived in light, portable houses that were easy to pack around.

They would return to their winter homes before the first snowfall.

Oh, the stories – never have I heard such stories before.

There was one story that I really liked, I guess because it was so unbelievable but at the same time, very well told. It's the story of the water spirit."

Well, I bolted up right away, and asked, "Grandpa, did you say, water spirit?"

He smiled and nodded. I'm pretty sure my eyes almost popped right out of my head.

"Indeed, I did. In the stories I was told while living with the syilx, the water spirit has two forms; one is spiritual and the other form is physical.

You see, water is so sacred to the syilx for many reasons. To name just one of those reasons that I'll remember for the rest of my life, is the lesson it carries.

"How does water carry lessons, grandpa?"

"Well, water reminds us not to be selfish, because whatever we do upstream affects anyone or anything downstream.

We could not survive without water, and it cleans us and connects us."

Well, that gave me a lot to think about. I thought water was just, well, water.

"It is a beautiful story – or it was, that is until the white people arrived." Grandpa thought for a moment, then continued.

"Once the white people arrived, the stories shifted from that of the water spirit to the stories about the lake monster."

"Wait. Grandpa, *we* are the white people, aren't we? What did we do?"

"Well, it wasn't until the white people arrived on the lands, that the stories about the lake monster began." I shivered.

"Until then, there was never any such thing as a lake monster. So, did the stories become twisted to become one story?

I think over time, they may have.

What my personal belief is, that the lake is home to not one, but two different entities.

One is the sacred water spirit, and the second is the lake monster." Now I was really confused.

"Grandpa, how can you believe in different things at once about the same thing?"

"Because what I saw could not have been a sacred spirit of the water. What I saw was evil, and it could only have been a monster. The lake monster."

Grandpa was dead serious, I could tell. And I also could tell, that he was ready to tell me the rest of his story.

"I woke early one morning, and headed out to the lake, alone. I wanted to catch some fish to bring back to the villagers.

I had become quite good at fishing, and hoped to come back with a bounty, enough to feed everyone.

It didn't quite turn out that way.

I reached the shore, and slipped off my boots, rolled up my trousers and waded into the water. The lake was as smooth as a sheet of glass. Not even a ripple on the surface.

I cast my net and was enjoying the quiet

of the dawn, and I recall that I was also counting my blessings.

You see, my cup is always half full."

I still didn't know what that meant, but the story was really getting good, now.

"So, the morning was quiet and peaceful. I kept very still so as not to scare off the fish while casting my net.

I stayed that way for about an hour, and I caught not even one fish.

I'm not the kind of person to give up easily, but when I realized how long I'd been standing in the lake without a nibble, I began to take better note of my surroundings.

Birds that would ordinarily chirp, were not chirping. The air was still and silent. No rustling in the brush around the lake, meaning wildlife, for reasons known only to them, had headed for the hills, far away from the water.

It felt like time stood still. The only thing I could clearly hear, was my breathing in, breathing out, and I think the sound of my own heart beating.

I didn't know what was going on.

I looked over the water, and far off in the distance, I saw a canoe slowly making its way across.

All of a sudden, water began splashing up to my knees.

Well, the canoe itself was not at all big enough to cause that kind of a disturbance in the lake.

Before I knew it, I was soaked up to my waist. I looked back toward the canoe, and just then, I saw a giant tail whip up fast out of the water and in the next moment, slammed down, right beside the canoe.

Even though I was a great distance away, the impact of the tail against the water caused enormous waves to reach the shore, and I was thrown right off my feet.

I landed flat on my back in the lake.

Once I gathered my senses and choked and spat out a whole lot of water, I saw that I'd lost my only net.

There wasn't a trace of it, anywhere. I then looked off in the distance and tried to spot the canoe, and like my net, it was just gone."

"Grandpa! What did you see?"

"It was the lake monster. I couldn't believe what I was seeing, and I was terrified. It had been too far away to tell what colour it was, but I could surely see the shape.

In all, the beast was at least 40 feet long – I could tell because every 4 feet or so, parts of it, like camel humps, raised from the water as it slithered toward the canoe.

Avery, it all happened in about as fast as the blink of an eye.

You can guess, that I returned to the village, soaking wet, and without any fish."

"Yes. Did you tell anyone in the village what you saw?" Grandpa shook his head.

"No. I didn't want to bother or upset anyone. The syilx people firmly believe in the sacred water spirit, and it was not up to me to tell them anything different.

It wasn't just that. The syilx are a highly respected people and their beliefs have been passed down from generation to generation.

We are talking about thousands of years of having the sacred spirit of the water being an important part of their lives.

Because I saw what I saw, I do believe that Okanagan Lake is home to both the water spirit, in two forms, and the lake monster."

I don't think I would have told anyone, either.

"But Avery, what I saw was not rare. I had heard other stories about the lake monster, too.

One story is about a visiting chief and his family; they were crossing the lake, when the same sort of thing happened and canoe and all, they all just disappeared.

Another story years later, about a settler that was crossing with his horses tethered to the back of his canoe... he had to cut loose the horses.

He and his canoe survived, but his horses were never seen again.

In each instance, it has been said that the lake monster felt only negative or angry energy from the chief, his family, and from the settler years later.

Their bad energy attracted similar energy,

causing the disappearance of the chief and his family.

It was only because of the settler's quick thinking and sharp blade, that he made it to shore."

"Grandpa, is that like treat others how you want to be treated? Except it's treat water how you would like water to treat you?"

"Exactly, Avery. Since those days, the lake monster has been seen many, many times by a lot of different people.

In the early 1920s, and by the white people, it was given the name, Ogopogo.

But, I know for a fact, that Ogopogo has no connection at all to the beautiful spirit of the water."

"How? I don't understand what you mean, grandpa."

I wondered how many good and evil

spirits might live in Lake Okanagan. I asked him just that.

"There is no such thing as evil or good spirits within the syilx beliefs. Their belief lies in the power we give something.

So, if we went into the water, maybe for a swim, and were feeling respect, calm and happy, the water would respond calmly.

But, if we went into the water feeling angry, we could expect the water to react angrily."

Grandpa must have seen my eyebrows wrinkle together.

"Well, this might be one of the things that we don't understand or explain. We didn't grow up learning this and so I'm not sure we could ever completely understand.

But, as I've said, the water spirit has two forms.

The spiritual form has the body of a serpent, the head of a horse and the antlers of a deer."

No kidding, I really did not understand, even though I wanted to and tried.

"The physical form is the water, itself. When the waters act wild, that brings joy to the syilx because it means that the water spirit is happily playing.

Believing what I believe, what is now Ogopogo should never be confused with the water spirit in either form.

The water spirit would never behave in such a way to cause harm to people.

I could write a book, Avery, describing all that I learned during my time with the syilx."

This was a whole lot of information for me to swallow. Before this night, they were just stories to me.

But now I knew that they had never, ever been just stories to my grandpa.

"Grandpa, how does the traveling work?" I didn't understand at all.

"Well, boy. I don't know how it works. I just know that it does, and I accept that.

Just remember that once you've taken a coin, you must keep that coin right with you, until you're ready to come back home.

You can't lose the coin, or you might never return." How scary would that be, I thought.

"But how long were you with the syilx people? If you learned all those things and even saw a monster, it sounds like you were gone for a very long time."

It did not make any sense to me. For all I knew, grandpa was never away for very long. Maybe a couple of days at a time, or so.

"I spent about 6 years with them."

Grandpa saw the look on my face.

"Avery, it's one of the things that can't be explained.

I'm telling you all of this to prepare you. This is part of your training, so that when it's your turn to keep the coins, you'll know to expect the unexpected.

My dad trained me, when I was a few years older than you.

When I travel, time means nothing here at home. For example, the six years that I spent with the syilx, your mom was three years old, a little bit of a thing.

I had finished having breakfast before I left, and I returned that same day, just in time for supper.

Now off you go back to the house for bed, and we'll train some more tomorrow after school."

It was past my bedtime when I washed up, brushed my teeth and climbed under the covers.

I could barely sleep a wink. I couldn't wait to go back to the shed the next day.

When I did finally fall asleep, my dreams were full of lake monsters. Not just one lake monster, but many; I'm sure, a dozen lake monsters.

In my dream, my grandpa bravely fought them all off and scared them away with his sword.

To be continued....

(the above images of the 1911 Canadian silver dollar are the property of the **Royal Mint Museum** and are used with permission)

EXTRA READING
The following information has been generously provided to
the author, by the
Bank of Canada Museum

Historical Value

The historic value of the 1911 silver dollar pattern is without comparison. In 1910, the Laurier government introduced legislation to mint a Canadian silver dollar after a petition was presented in the House of Commons by Members of Parliament from British Columbia to as part of the amendments to the *Currency Act*. People in the west preferred coins to notes, and officials believed that a large Canadian coin should replace American silver dollars, which were in extensive use in the West. While it was generally agreed that notes were preferable to large coins, amendments to the Currency Act were passed in parliament, and the new silver dollar would be made of sterling silver.

In November 1910, Dr. James Bonar, master of the Royal Canadian Mint, placed an order with the Royal Mint in London for a pair of master dies to strike the dollar. The master dies had to be made in England because Canada did not yet have the facilities to hub dies. In the spring of 1911, new machinery was acquired to mint the dollar coin and the blanks were ready for striking. The master dies were late on arriving in Ottawa and according to the Royal Canadian Mint's annual report for 1911, "no dollars were struck." No explanation was offered; however, it is believed that new Unionist government of Sir Robert Borden who was voted into power in the September 1911 ordered the cancellation of the project. The master dies for the 1911 dollar were finally delivered in November but were never used. A lead pattern of the coin was delivered with the dies. Today, the 1911 silver dollar is nicknamed the "Emperor of Canadian Coins" by the numismatic community.

Historically, the 1911 silver dollar's existence tells us something about circulating specie in Canada. The 1911 dollar was proposed to offset the presence of American silver dollars on the West Coast in view of the preference of British Columbians for coins rather than paper, the reason for this is not well known. The existence of the 1911 dollar and the circumstances of its production offer an opportunity for research into the monetary conditions in British Columbia at the end of the nineteenth and the beginning of the twentieth centuries.

***

EXTRA READING

This information has been generously provided to the author, by the
Sncəwips Heritage Museum

The Sncəwips Heritage Museum has been most generous, in not only providing cultural and historical information for the purpose of this book, but also correcting a few discrepancies and unknowns contained in the first draft. I am forever grateful for our numerous communications in order to make the factual elements in the story, as accurate as possible.

Arrival in the Okanagan Valley

In the first draft of the story, I had grandpa arriving in the Okanagan Valley in 1875. Well, that could very well have happened, except the rest of the story wouldn't have.

If grandpa arrived in the 1870s he would not have had the opportunity to befriend the syilx people. In 1876, the *Indian Act* was in force, which resulted in, among many other inhumane atrocities, removing the First Nations people from their native lands and forcing them to live on reserves. As such, the syilx were not allowed to leave the reserves without written permission, and grandpa would certainly not have brought them fish. In doing so, he would have faced arrest.

qwiċi houses
These were pit homes that were 4 to 5 feet deep in the ground, and some were large enough to fit 4 generations of people. There were two entrances; a tunnel for the women and elders, and a log ladder that would go from the floor to a hole in the top of the home for the men to use.

The syilx were semi-nomadic. When they would leave their winter homes during the warmer months, they used portable homes made from tule reeds.

Fishing
The syilx indeed fished with nets, that were created from a plant fibre called spiċən

(pronounced, "spee-ts-en") which is the hemp fibre of the dogbane plant. Three pronged spears, dip nets and weirs were also used to fish.

One story told by the elders, is that back then, the salmon were abundant; so plentiful in fact, that during the salmon runs, the rivers would turn red, and that one could actually cross the river by walking across the backs of the salmon.

I say heartfelt, "lim limt" to the syilx people, which translates to, "thank you" in my language.

***

ABOUT THE AUTHOR

The author lives in the beautiful Cowichan Valley on Vancouver Island, British Columbia. She is pleased to present the Coinkeeper Series and very much looks forward to introducing you to grandpa's friends, Patty and Bell, in the next book.

For more information, please visit:
www.teresaschapansky.com

Manufactured by Amazon.ca
Bolton, ON

18071443R00028